THE PERFECT THANKSGIVING

BY EILEEN SPINELLI

ILLUSTRATED BY JOANN ADINOLFI

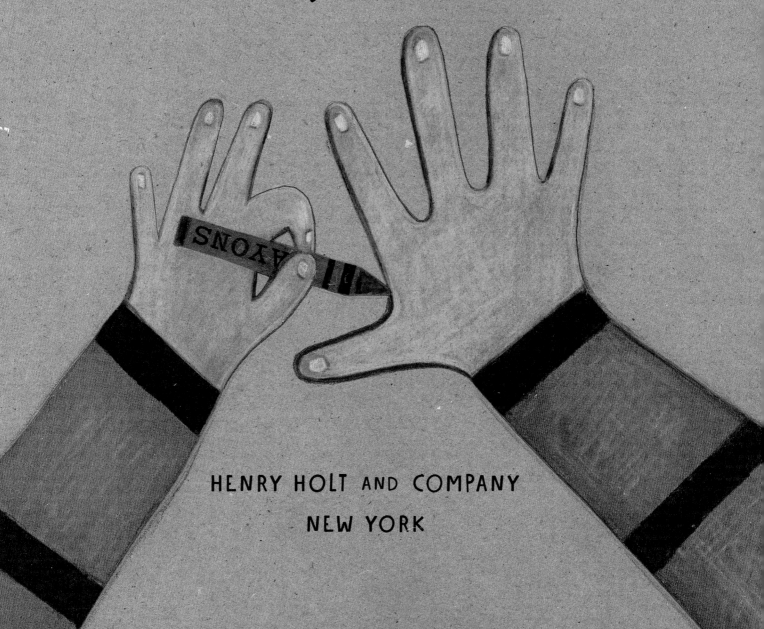

HENRY HOLT AND COMPANY

NEW YORK

For Eileen and Jim Nechas,
friends for whom I am thankful —E.S.

For Karsten, Hans-Liam, and
Gemma Sofia—I am thankful for you —J.A.

HURRY!

Henry Holt and Company, LLC
Publishers since 1866
115 West 18th Street, New York, New York 10011
www.henryholt.com

Library of Congress Cataloging-in-Publication Data
Spinelli, Eileen. The perfect Thanksgiving / by Eileen Spinelli ; illustrated by JoAnn Adinolfi.
Summary: Two families—one that is perfect and one that is far from it—celebrate Thanksgiving in their own loving ways.
[1. Thanksgiving Day–Fiction. 2. Family life–Fiction. 3. Stories in rhyme.] I. Adinolfi, JoAnn, ill. II. Title.
PZ8.3.S759 Pe 2003   [E]–dc21   2002010859   ISBN 0-8050-6531-8 / First Edition–2003 / Designed by Donna Mark
Printed in the United States of America on acid-free paper. ∞ 10 9 8 7 6 5 4 3 2 1

The artist used gouache, colored pencil, and collage on craft paper to create the illustrations for this book.

O3023 2118

Abigail Archer's mother
wears organdy and pearls.
She decorates their homemade pies
with fancy whipped-cream swirls.

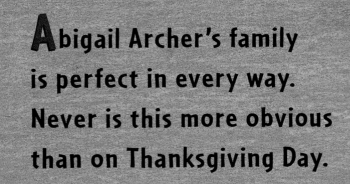

Abigail Archer's family
is perfect in every way.
Never is this more obvious
than on Thanksgiving Day.

TURN THE PAGE
AND TAKE A
LOOK!

Abigail Archer's father
serves white meat all around.
Everyone takes dainty bites,
and no one makes a sound.

CHEW

CHOMP

My grandpa chews the gizzards.
My brother chomps the wings.
My sister slurps. My uncle burps.
And Aunt Clarissa sings.

SLURP

Abigail's older cousins
read books in velvet chairs.
The younger ones bring favorite toys,
and everybody shares.

My mother's dressed in blue jeans.
Her pies are from the store.
Her Jell-O mold, a-quivering,
a-quivers to the floor!

After dinner at Abigail's,
after the dishes are done,
some of the grown-ups take a walk.
Others play chess for fun.

After dinner at our house,
the dogs sneak off with scraps.
Some of the grown-ups watch TV.
Others take long naps.

My family and the Archers
are different—this I know.
We can't tell peas from green legumes
or snails from escargots.

But we're alike in one way,
the nicest way by far—
alike in just how loving
our different families are.